Blastoff! Readers are carefully developed by literacy experts to build reading stamina and move students toward fluency by combining standards-based content with developmentally appropriate text.

LEVELS

 Level 1 provides the most support through repetition of high-frequency words, light text, predictable sentence patterns, and strong visual support.

 Level 2 offers early readers a bit more challenge through varied sentences, increased text load, and text-supportive special features.

 Level 3 advances early-fluent readers toward fluency through increased text load, less reliance on photos, advancing concepts, longer sentences, and more complex special features.

★ **Blastoff! Universe**

Reading Level

 Grade K

 Grades 1–3

 Grade 4

This edition first published in 2022 by Bellwether Media, Inc.

No part of this publication may be reproduced in whole or in part without written permission of the publisher. For information regarding permission, write to Bellwether Media, Inc., Attention: Permissions Department, 6012 Blue Circle Drive, Minnetonka, MN 55343.

Library of Congress Cataloging-in-Publication Data

Names: Duling, Kaitlyn, author.
Title: Airplanes / by Kaitlyn Duling.
Description: Minneapolis, MN : Bellwether Media, Inc., 2022. | Series: Blastoff! Readers: How it works | Includes bibliographical references and index. | Audience: Ages 5-8 | Audience: Grades 2-3 | Summary: "Simple text and full-color photography introduce beginning readers to how airplanes work. Developed by literacy experts for students in kindergarten through third grade"-- Provided by publisher.
Identifiers: LCCN 2021049250 (print) | LCCN 2021049251 (ebook) | ISBN 9781644875971 (library binding) | ISBN 9781648346729 (paperback) | ISBN 9781648346088 (ebook)
Subjects: LCSH: Airplanes--Juvenile literature. | CYAC: Airplanes.
Classification: LCC TL547 .D78 2022 (print) | LCC TL547 (ebook) | DDC 629.133/34--dc23/eng/20211103
LC record available at https://lccn.loc.gov/2021049250
LC ebook record available at https://lccn.loc.gov/2021049251

Text copyright © 2022 by Bellwether Media, Inc. BLASTOFF! READERS and associated logos are trademarks and/or registered trademarks of Bellwether Media, Inc.

Editor: Betsy Rathburn   Series Design: Jeffrey Kollock   Book Designer: Gabriel Hilger

Printed in the United States of America, North Mankato, MN.

Table of Contents

What Are Airplanes?	4
How Do Airplanes Work?	6
The Future of Airplanes	18
Glossary	22
To Learn More	23
Index	24

What Are Airplanes?

Airplanes are machines that fly through the air. They are much faster than other ways of traveling.

Businesses use airplanes to send items to countries around the world. People use airplanes to travel quickly!

How Do Airplanes Work?

Airplanes carry people, goods, and fuel. These add a lot of weight to airplanes.

The weight must be spread out evenly. This helps planes stay balanced. When everything is loaded, it is time to fly!

fueling an airplane

loading an airplane

Airplanes need big engines to fly. The engines let off **exhaust**. This creates **thrust**. Spinning **propellers** create thrust, too.

propeller

engine ➡

exhaust ➡

Thrust pushes the plane forward. The plane speeds down the runway. Takeoff!

fuselage

Drag slows planes down. It is caused by wind pushing against the plane.

Planes are built to cut down on drag. Most have a long, narrow **fuselage**. This helps the plane cut through the air!

Parts of an Airplane

Airplane wings are tilted up to direct the airflow. This leads to more **pressure** on the bottom of the wings.

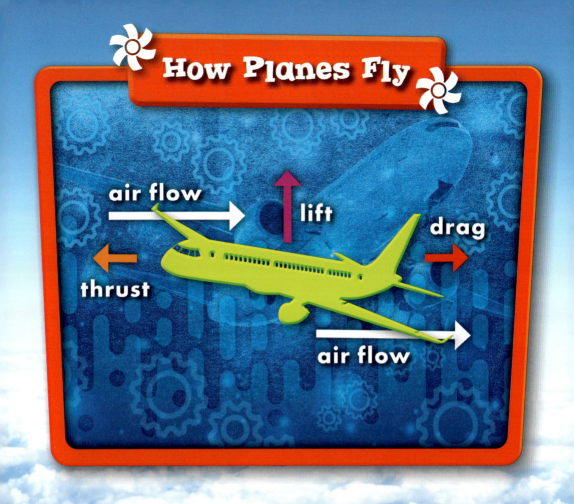

This creates **lift**. It helps planes stay in the air!

The pilot steers from inside the plane. They move **ailerons** on the plane's wings. Ailerons make the plane **roll** left and right.

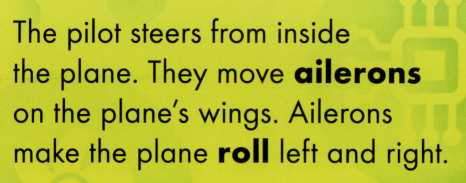

aileron

rolling

Steering A Plane

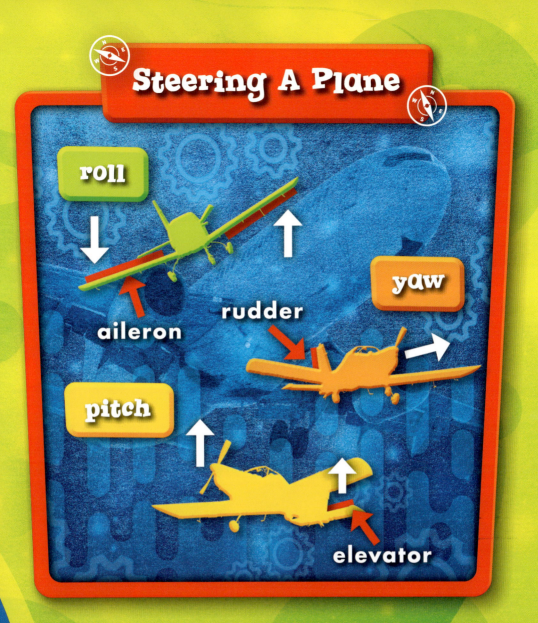

The **rudder** controls the plane's **yaw**. It turns the plane's nose left and right.

Elevators near the tail let the pilot control **pitch**. They make the plane go up and down.

When elevators move up, the plane's nose goes up. When they move down, the nose goes down.

elevator

The Future of Airplanes

electric plane

Today's planes use fuel. But electric airplanes may be used in the future.

Electric planes do not use fuel. They are quieter and cause less **pollution**.

pollution

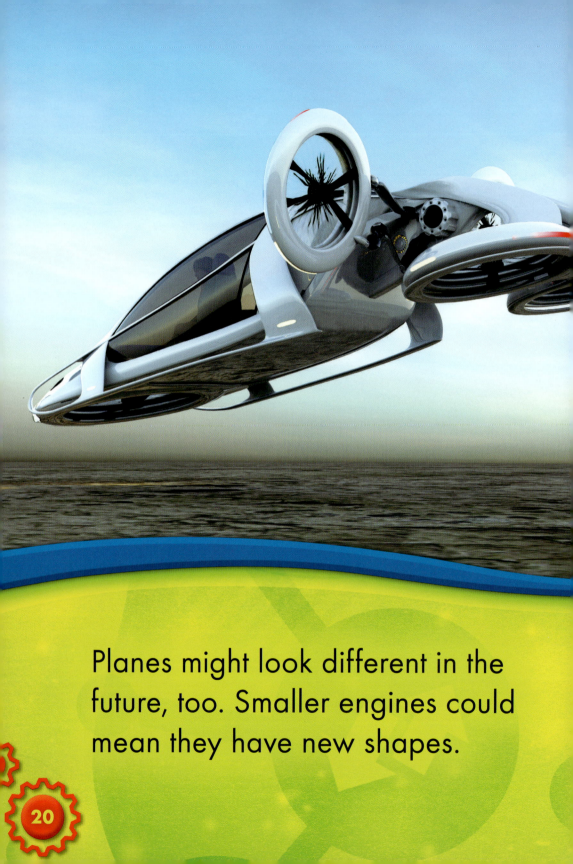

Planes might look different in the future, too. Smaller engines could mean they have new shapes.

Question

What do you think future planes will look like?

Narrow, V-shaped planes could fly faster. What new heights will planes reach next? The sky is the limit!

Glossary

ailerons—parts of an airplane's wings that control the plane's roll

drag—a force that slows down motion

elevators—parts of an airplane that help control the plane's pitch

exhaust—the mixture of gases released by machines that burn fuel

fuselage—the main body of an airplane

lift—a force that holds an airplane in the air

pitch—the up and down movements of an airplane's nose

pollution—substances that make the earth dirty or unsafe

pressure—the weight or force that something makes when it pushes against something else

propellers—spinning parts that create thrust for an airplane

roll—the left and right spinning movements of an airplane

rudder—the part of an airplane that makes the plane turn left and right

thrust—the force that pushes something forward

yaw—the left and right movements of an airplane's nose

To Learn More

AT THE LIBRARY
Duling, Kaitlyn. *Cars*. Minneapolis, Minn.: Bellwether Media, 2022.

Fretland VanVoorst, Jenny. *Airplanes*. Minneapolis, Minn.: Jump!, 2018.

Mattern, Joanne. *We Go on an Airplane*. Egremont, Mass.: Red Chair Press, 2019.

ON THE WEB

FACTSURFER

Factsurfer.com gives you a safe, fun way to find more information.

1. Go to www.factsurfer.com.

2. Enter "airplanes" into the search box and click 🔍.

3. Select your book cover to see a list of related content.

Index

ailerons, 14
air, 4, 11, 12, 13
businesses, 5
drag, 10, 11
electric airplanes, 18, 19
elevators, 16
engines, 8, 20
exhaust, 8
fly, 4, 6, 8, 13, 21
fuel, 6, 18, 19
fuselage, 10, 11
future, 18, 20
goods, 6
how planes fly, 13
lift, 13
nose, 15, 16, 17
parts, 11
people, 5, 6
pilot, 14, 16
pitch, 16
pollution, 19

pressure, 12
propellers, 8
question, 21
roll, 14
rudder, 15
shapes, 20, 21
steers, 14, 15
tail, 16
thrust, 8, 9
travel, 4, 5
weight, 6
wind, 10
wings, 12, 14
yaw, 15

The images in this book are reproduced through the courtesy of: Caftor, front cover; phive, p. 3; Aerial-motion, pp. 4-5; Matej Kastelic, p. 5; Karolis Kavolelis, p. 6; Pierre-Yves Babelon, pp. 6-7; Corepics VOF, pp. 8-9; Caron Badkin, p. 8 (inset); Media_works, p. 9; IM_photo, pp. 10-11; brillenstimmer, p. 11; aapsky, pp. 12-13; Max Herman, pp. 14-15; steve estvanik, p. 14 (inset); Franco Agustin Ercolino, p. 16 (inset); Skycolors, pp. 16-17; Philipp Hayer, pp. 18-19; Matti Blume, p. 19; VanderWolf Images, p. 19 (inset); kolesinibimitresku, pp. 20-21; Sergey Ogaryov, p. 23.